Spuds

Spuds

by KAREN HESSE

Illustrated by WENDY WATSON

SCHOLASTIC PRESS · NEW YORK

The night me and Maybelle and Eddie harvested potatoes,
Ma was workin' night shift.
Our ma, she's mighty fine,
but lately it seems like she got nothin' left over,
not even for us kids.

My big sister, Maybelle,

she's always plannin' and schemin'.

She'd been watchin' Mr. Kenney's harvester for days.

"Jack," she said. "I'm thinkin' we need a tater harvest of our own,

and tonight looks just about right for it."

"Ma's been workin' so hard," Maybelle said.

"Let's bring her in some extra.

'Less we gather them spuds off Kenney's field,

they'll go to rot, sure thing,

and that's just plain wasteful. Ain't that right, Eddie?"

Little old Eddie,

he just dotes on Maybelle, I don't know why.

That boy hooked his big eyes on Maybelle's face and said,

"M-m-m."

So when Ma left for work, me and Maybelle,

we layered on a heap a' clothes. Maybelle said,

"Jack, you get the wagon out of the shed while I dress Eddie."

"I ain't messin' in that shed with all them spiders and things," I said.

"You get the wagon, Maybelle."

But she didn't.

Just 'cause I'm in the middle I gotta do whatever Maybelle says.

Me and Maybelle, we folded up three old sacks

and put them between Eddie's bottom and the rusty wagon bed.

Eddie wore his hat with the earflaps.

He held on to the wagon sides and grinned.

We three kids headed out Waddell Road in that rattle-bang fashion.
Maybelle, she goosed us with the meals Ma'd make out'a them spuds.
"You'll see. Ma's gonna boil 'em, and bake 'em. She's gonna
slice 'em thin as fingernails and fry 'em up crusty brown with
lots of salt sparklin'."
Man, my mouth juiced up just thinkin' about it.

We left the road and stole into Kenney's field,

creepin' over the clawed-up earth,

our hands feelin' for night spuds.

And there was dozens of 'em, just like Maybelle said.

Me and Maybelle, we got a pretty good rhythm going
picking up spuds,
when some high-beam car came flying 'round the bend.
Maybelle, just like that, she vanished into a ditch.
Like a couple of woodchucks, me and Eddie dove, too.

That car whizzed right past us.

We stayed down,

three tater-snatchers,

flat-bellied in the dirt,

till the tire buzz faded. Then,

rising up in the moonlight,

we commenced to cockadoodlin',

revelin' in the pure pleasure of a close call.

Every now and then I picked up a piece of tater too small to keep.

Them slivers a' spuds, they was just right for flipping at my sister.

And sure, I tossed one. But Maybelle, she didn't lob it back. Nope.

She called out, "Don't you be wastin' them spuds, Jack."

So I dropped the rest inside my sack

thinkin' on how they'd taste cooked up,

fillin' me with all kinds of goodness.

We nearly froze stiff under that travelin' moon.

Frost glittered everywhere.

Finally, Maybelle said, "Jack, we got enough.

Let's get on home and put Eddie to bed."

And Eddie, asleep on his feet, whispered, "M-m-m."

I pulled the wagon with Eddie curled inside,
blissful in the moonlight.
Bringing up the rear, Maybelle trudged,
like an old mule,
dragging them tater sacks behind her.

When we got home,

Maybelle tucked Eddie in

while I spilled the first bag open across the kitchen floor.

Them hard spuds rolled out,

fillin' the room with the smell of dirt.

I bent down to sort the muddy clumps.

Then I knelt.

Then I sat down in the middle of the cracked linoleum.

And that's when I felt a hole open up inside my heart.

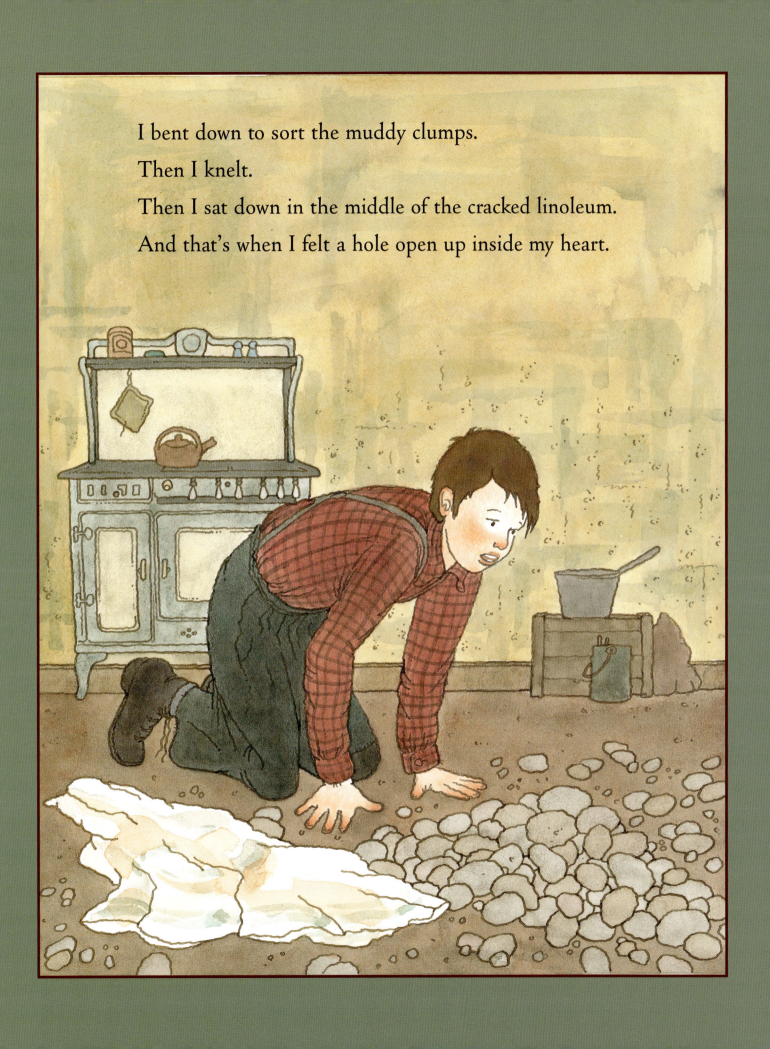

Maybelle crouched down beside me.

"What's eatin' you, Jack?"

"These ain't potatoes, Maybelle.

They're *stones*!

We been harvestin' stones!"

One sack after another revealed the same sad truth.
In the end, after emptying all three bags,
we came up with one short stack of potatoes —
all the rest was rock.

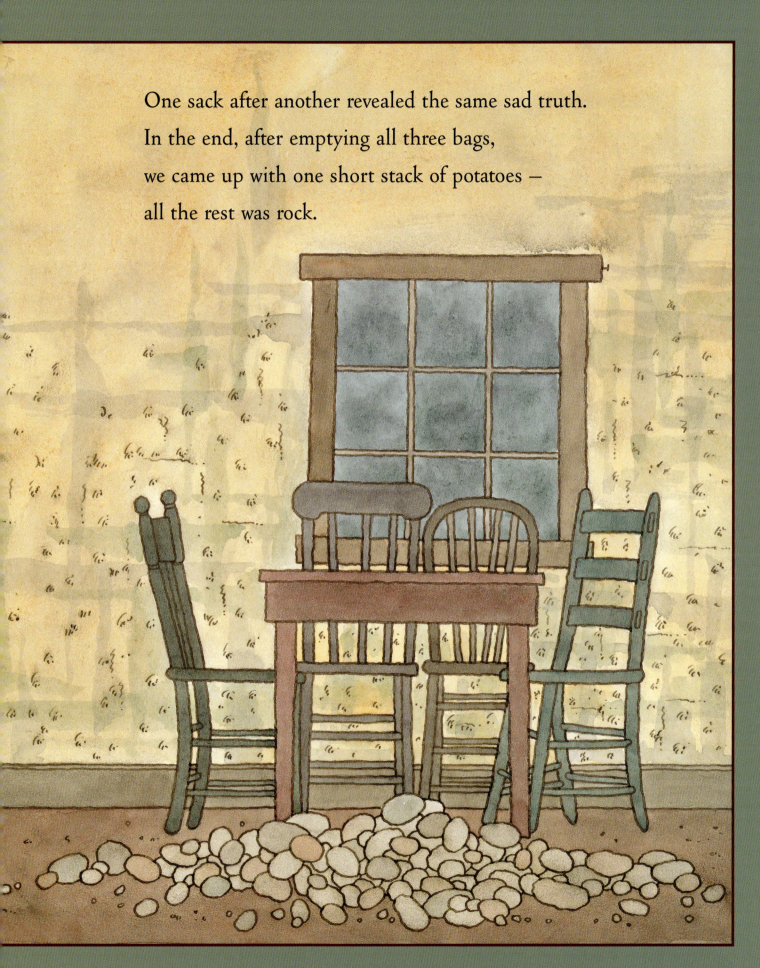

Sitting at the kitchen table,

chewin' on dirt,

it felt like me and Maybelle and Eddie,

we was just three little no 'count kids,

worth about nothing to no one.

And to make matters worse,

when Ma got home and found out what we'd done,

she wasn't pleased at all. Said we was grounded,

startin' as soon as we got back from Mr. Kenney's,

where we was to return all we'd taken.

That Mr. Kenney, we had to chase him down to make him listen.

But he sure chuckled when he heard us out.

Said we done him a favor. Said he was mighty glad to have them stones clear of his field.

"Next year after harvest," he said, "you kids come on back and sack up as many rocks as you like. Any taters you happen to glean in the process, they're yours to keep. You tell your ma I said that, you hear?"

And them sacks didn't feel half so heavy coming back home,
what with Mr. Kenney and his kindness.
We told Ma all he'd said.

And Maybelle, she owned as how we'd only gone after them spuds
so Ma wouldn't have to work so hard,
and Ma, that's about when she pulled on her tatty old robe and
commenced to making the biggest fry-up you ever did see.

In our tumble-down kitchen,

we hooked our big eyes on Ma's back,

breathing in that good fried smell.

And Ma, she served up heaps of pan-crisp potatoes,

leaning over us,

her sweet smile pouring down.

And I knew right then,
our ma, she loved us big,
so big that love of hers could turn
even three little spuds like us
into something mighty fine.

Maybelle tugged at Ma's robe.

"These here little rocks you fried up, Ma?

Why, they are truly good enough to eat.

Ain't that right, Eddie?"

And Eddie, his grubby fist clutching his fork,

his mouth filled with all kinds of goodness, said,

"M-m-m."

For my brother, Barry
mmm . . . mmm . . . mmm
— K. H.

With thanks to Spudniks everywhere, particularly Beryl and Donna Kenney, Naamon and
Miriam King, Neil Pelsue, Randy Hesse, Wendy Watson, and, of course, Dianne Hess.

For my children
— W. W.

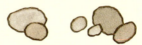

Text Copyright © 2008 by Karen Hesse · Illustrations Copyright © 2008 by Wendy Watson

Library of Congress Cataloging-in-Publication Data

Hesse, Karen.
Spuds / by Karen Hesse; illustrated by Wendy Watson.—1st ed.
p. cm.
Summary: Maybelle, Jack, and Eddie want to help Ma by putting something extra on the table,
so they set out in the dark to take potatoes from a nearby field, but when they arrive home and
empty their potato sacks, they are surprised by what they find.
[1. Potatoes—Fiction. 2. Country life—Fiction. 3. Brothers and sisters—Fiction.]
I. Watson, Wendy, ill. II. Title.
PZ7.H4364Sp 2008
[E]—dc22 · 2007024046

ISBN-13: 978-0-439-87993-4 · ISBN-10: 0-439-87993-0

10 9 8 7 6 5 4 3 2 1   08 09 10 11 12

Printed in Singapore 46 · First edition, September 2008

The display type was set in P22 Pan Am · The text was set in Cloister Old Style
The art was created using pencil, colored ink, watercolor, and gouache on watercolor paper.
Book design by Elizabeth B. Parisi